*Acting Edition*

# The Tomb of King Tot

# King Tot

by Olivia Dufault

⫼SAMUEL FRENCH⫼

ISBN 978-0-573-70594-6

www.concordtheatricals.com
www.concordtheatricals.co.uk

---

**FOR PRODUCTION INQUIRIES**

UNITED STATES AND CANADA
info@concordtheatricals.com
1-866-979-0447

UNITED KINGDOM AND EUROPE
licensing@concordtheatricals.co.uk
020-7054-7298

Each title is subject to availability from Concord Theatricals Corp., depending upon country of performance. Please be aware that *THE TOMB OF KING TOT* may not be licensed by Concord Theatricals Corp. in your territory. Professional and amateur producers should contact the nearest Concord Theatricals Corp. office or licensing partner to verify availability.

---

This work is published by Samuel French, an imprint of Concord Theatricals Corp.

### MUSIC AND THIRD-PARTY MATERIALS USE NOTE

Licensees are solely responsible for obtaining formal written permission from copyright owners to use copyrighted music and/or other copyrighted third-party materials (e.g. artworks, logos) in the performance of this play and are strongly cautioned to do so. If no such permission is obtained by the licensee, then the licensee must use only original music and materials that the licensee owns and controls. Licensees are solely responsible and liable for clearances of all third-party copyrighted materials, including without limitation music, and shall indemnify the copyright owners of the play(s) and their licensing agent, Concord Theatricals Corp., against any costs, expenses, losses and liabilities arising from the use of such copyrighted third-party materials by licensees. For music, please contact the appropriate music licensing authority in your territory for the rights to any incidental music.

### IMPORTANT BILLING AND CREDIT REQUIREMENTS

If you have obtained performance rights to this title, please refer to your licensing agreement for important billing and credit requirements.

***THE TOMB OF KING TOT*** was initially produced by Clubbed Thumb (Maria Striar, Artistic Director). It was directed by Portia Krieger, with scenic design by Carolyn Mraz, costume design by Tilly Grimes, lighting design by Barbara Samuels, and sound design by Lee Kinney. The Production Stage Manager was Corinn Moreno. The cast was as follows:

**JANE HALEY/MUMMY** . . . . . . . . . . . . . . . . . . . . . . . . . . . Annie McNamara

**ATLANTA/KING TOT** . . . . . . . . . . . . . . . . . . . . . . . . . . . . . Bianca Crudo

**PORTER/HOREMHEB** . . . . . . . . . . . . . . . . . . . . . . . . . . . . . Nick Choksi

**KISSY CANDIDA/CROCODILE-WOMAN** . . . . . . . . . . Carmen M. Herlihy

**LIONEL FEATHER/ANUBIS** . . . . . . . . . . . . . . . . . . . . . . . . . Brad Bellamy

# CHARACTERS

**JANE HALEY** – F, late-thirties, cartoonist
**MUMMY** – F, mummy

**ATLANTA** – F, teenage girl
**KING TOT** – F, Egyptian boy-king

**PORTER** – M, late-thirties, stepfather
**HOREMHEB** – M, Egyptian slave

**KISSY CANDIDA** – F, late-thirties, cartoonist
**CROCODILE-WOMAN** – F, crocodile-woman

**LIONEL FEATHER** – M, early-sixties, cartoonist
**ANUBIS** – M, jackal-headed God of the Dead

# SETTING

A mixture of a lower-middle-class New England living room and a cartoon-like version of Ancient Egypt.

# AUTHOR'S NOTES

Characters listed together are played by the same actor.

## Scene One

*(Onstage is a construct with three open panels that one can stand in. Above the first panel are the words "King Tot," and beneath it, "by Jane Haley." It resembles an enormous three-panel comic strip that one can walk inside. In Panel One stand* **KING TOT** *and* **HOREMHEB**. *They stand immobile in this panel, until they move on to the next panel and assume a different position. It should seem as if we're reading a weekday newspaper comic strip.* **JANE** *works at her drawing station.)*

*(Panel One.)*

**KING TOT.** Horemheb! This is my kingdom and I demand it be given a new name!

**HOREMHEB.** But King Tot, it has always been known as Egypt –

*(Panel Two.)*

**KING TOT.** From now on, it shall be known as Me-gypt.

**HOREMHEB.** Me-gypt?

*(Panel Three.)*

**KING TOT.** After all, the gods say I am ageless!

**HOREMHEB.** But you're only nine years old!

*(Next comic.)*

*(Panel One.)*

But King Tot, if we replace all of the sands with precious jewels, won't it hurt your feet?

**KING TOT.** Send for my slaves! I need a new pair of sandals!

*(Panel Two.)*

**HOREMHEB.** The slaves will build the sandals?

7

**KING TOT**. Stupid Horemheb, the slaves will *be* the sandals!

 *(Panel Three.)*

**HOREMHEB**. What're you gonna call those contraptions?!

**KING TOT**. Man-dals!

 *(Next comic.)*

 *(Panel One.)*

Horemheb, I demand you fill my bath with milk and money!

**HOREMHEB**. But sire, that will irritate your precious skin…

 *(Panel Two.)*

**KING TOT**. Horemheb…

**HOREMHEB**. Oh no, here we go again…

 *(Panel Three.)*

**KING TOT**. I WANT MY MUMMY!

 *(The force of **KING TOT**'s tantrum propels **HOREMHEB** offstage. **KING TOT** storms out. **JANE** proudly examines her comic strip. **ATLANTA** enters with her backpack. She's wearing heavy eye makeup – the same as **KING TOT**'s, and a long-sleeved shirt that covers her arms. **ATLANTA** begins to go to her room.)*

**JANE**. Wait. How was school?

**ATLANTA**. Good.

**JANE**. Nothing interesting happened?

**ATLANTA**. No.

**JANE**. Nothing at all?

**ATLANTA**. A boy shat himself, but boys shit themselves all the time, so.

**JANE**. Huh. Super interesting. Hey, show me your arm.

**ATLANTA**. What?

**JANE**. I'd like you to show me your arm.

 *(**ATLANTA** lifts her arm. She points at it.)*

Lift up the sleeve.

ATLANTA. Yeah, I'm not doing that.

JANE. Your teacher called me again today.

ATLANTA. For phone sex?

JANE. Atlanta –

ATLANTA. What? I think your voice would be good for phone sex. That's what I tell people you do, actually. Everyone's really impressed.

JANE. I know what you did. And I'd like you to show me your arm.

ATLANTA. What did I do? I want you to tell me exactly what I did.

*(Beat.)*

JANE. Your teacher said you were coloring on your arm with a Sharpie in class.

ATLANTA. Okay.

JANE. And then, the Sharpie ran out of ink. So you took out another Sharpie. And began coloring on your arm again. And then that one died. And you took out another. Do I have to continue?

ATLANTA. Yes, please.

JANE. And at that point, he said, the smell was beginning to distract the other students.

ATLANTA. Uh-huh.

JANE. And apparently it got so bad that the girl sitting next to you threw up.

ATLANTA. She's bulimic anyway.

JANE. And then another girl threw up –

ATLANTA. Everyone's bulimic, a little bit.

JANE. Show me your arm.

*(Beat.* ATLANTA *pulls up her sleeve. Her arm is covered in black Sharpie ink.)*

You probably have ink poisoning.

ATLANTA. Probably.

*(ATLANTA takes out an enormous amount of Sharpie markers from her backpack.)*

ATLANTA. Sharpies can color over anything, you know. And once it's in, it never comes out. If they hadn't stopped me? I would've colored my entire skin. I would've colored my eyes. I would've colored my lips. I would've colored my teeth and tongue. These taste really good, actually. Do you want one?

JANE. …I think you need to start talking to that therapist again.

ATLANTA. She's not actually a therapist.

JANE. Okay, she's not actually a therapist, but she used to be a therapist –

ATLANTA. She lives in a nursing home. She thought I was her mother. She said I was ruining her sex life.

JANE. Okay! Well, I don't know what exactly you want, but therapists are expensive, and –

ATLANTA. I want a siphon.

JANE. What?

ATLANTA. A siphon. Where do we keep the siphons?

JANE. Why do you want a siphon?

ATLANTA. It's for a school project with Tracy. I'm going to stay over at her house tonight.

JANE. No you're not. You're, I don't know, you're staying home and writing an apology to your teacher, and washing your arm, and –

ATLANTA. Do you ever get angry?

JANE. Of course I get angry! I'm currently angry!

ATLANTA. I don't think you're angry. Not really angry. Angry enough to tear off all your skin and reveal what you really are inside. And I think that makes you less of a woman. I think real women are the angriest animals on Earth.

JANE. …Well I think you're not a woman yet. So I think you actually have no idea what you're talking about. I know that you feel like this whole…thing you do is, I don't know, noble, or –

ATLANTA. It's not noble.

JANE. Excuse me?

ATLANTA. It's not noble. It's pathetic and weak.

*(Beat.)*

So you're not letting me go to Tracy's then?

JANE. No.

ATLANTA. Okay.

*(ATLANTA begins walking to her room.)*

JANE. Wait. If I let you stay at Tracy's. Will you promise me something?

ATLANTA. What?

JANE. Will you promise me that you won't do these stunts anymore?

ATLANTA. …Okay.

JANE. Okay.

ATLANTA. …So I should go?

JANE. Do you want to go?

ATLANTA. …Yes.

JANE. Then you should go.

ATLANTA. …Okay. Goodbye, then.

JANE. Goodbye.

*(ATLANTA begins to exit.)*

You're a teenager. That's all this is. I promise you.

ATLANTA. I don't think I'm actually a teenager. I think time works differently for me. I think I might be thousands of years old.

*(ATLANTA exits. JANE goes back to working. KING TOT and HOREMHEB enter.)*

*(Panel One.)*

KING TOT. Horemheb!! My camel is broken! It only has two humps!!

**HOREMHEB**. But sire, all camels have either one or two humps!

>*(Panel Two.)*

**KING TOT**. I deserve a camel with three humps! No four humps! No, ten humps!

>*(Panel Three.)*

**HOREMHEB**. Where will I find a camel like that??

**KING TOT**. At Hump Depot!

>*(Next comic.)*

>*(Panel One.)*

This is the Nile River, Horemheb.

**HOREMHEB**. Yes, sire.

>*(Panel Two.)*

**KING TOT**. I want you to stare at this spot in the river until you find me a crocodile. And then I want you to wrestle that crocodile for my amusement.

**HOREMHEB**. I'm getting too old for this…

>*(Panel Three.)*

**KING TOT**. Keep staring, Horemheb…

**HOREMHEB**. He's making me SEE-NILE!

>*(**KING TOT** and **HOREMHEB** exit. **PORTER** enters, sorting the mail.)*

**PORTER**. Hey, honey –

**JANE**. Hey, did you pass Atlanta on the way in?

**PORTER**. Oh, yeah! She, uh, she spit on me, actually?

**JANE**. She spit on you?!

**PORTER**. Yeah, and, uh, I kind of wanted to bring it up actually because…her spit…it landed on my shirt and…

>*(**PORTER** points to a part of his shirt that has black spit on it.)*

**JANE**. It's black…

**PORTER**. Yeah. And after she spit on me, she left to go, and I said, "I love you, Atlanta." And then she turned around. And she looked at me. And she said, "You'll never be my real dad. I love you too." And then she left. So I was thinking, maybe you should take her to the doctor? On account of her black spit?

**JANE**. Yeah.

> (**PORTER** *hands* **JANE** *the mail. She looks through it.*)

**PORTER**. She certainly is a tough little nut to crack. But you know, I was like that in my younger days. They called me "Tough Nut" –

> (**JANE** *stops. She stands and stares in awe at a letter.*)

**JANE**. Porter.

**PORTER**. Jane? What is it?

**JANE**. This letter. It's from Lionel Feather.

> *(Beat.)*

**PORTER**. Oh. Oh wow.

> *(Beat.)*

Who is Lionel Feather?

**JANE**. Who is Lionel Feather?! He writes "Packrats"! "Packrats"! The strip! About children! Living in a dump!

**PORTER**. The children live in a dump?

**JANE**. Yes! It's incredibly cute! I'm going to open. No I can't open. You open it. Oh my God.

> (**JANE** *hands him the letter and buries her head in her hands.*)

I can't breathe. Tell me what it says. I can't breathe.

**PORTER**. It says you're nominated for a…a chuckling willow?

> (**JANE** *looks up in awe.*)

**PORTER**. Jane?

**JANE**. ...I can't feel my face. The Chuckling Willow.

**PORTER**. I don't know what that it is, but I am so proud of you –

**JANE**. The Chuckling Willow is the single most important award for newspaper cartoonists in all of Eastern New England! Created by Lionel Feather, otherwise known as the Godfather of Light-Hearted Humor! The Laugh Master of New Hampshire! Mister Ha-Ha himself! Who else was nominated –

>    (**JANE** *reads the letter.*)

Dale Lovey! That's great, he's a totally untalented hack! Jeffica Newhart. Oh. Kissy Candida.

**PORTER**. You know her! I know her!

**JANE**. Yeah, she's great. So I need three months of unpublished work, that's fine –

>    (**JANE** *refers to her large stack of papers in the tray/box by her work station.*)

– And in exactly one week I have an interview at the Hilton Garden Inn with the one and only Giggle King, Lionel Feather! Hey, you know what we need right now, Porter? Wine! Get some from the basement!

**PORTER**. On it!

>    (**PORTER** *exits.* **JANE** *looks at the letter. She privately basks in it.* **PORTER** *returns with a bottle of wine.*)

What is this stuff? There are like cases and cases of it down there –

**JANE**. It's from Egypt! One of my readers from Wellfleet keeps sending them to me! It tastes terrible! I don't care! I want it! I want the terrible Egyptian wine, Porter! I feel like I'm unreal! I feel like I don't exist!

>    (**PORTER** *pours them both wine.*)

**PORTER**. Well, you deserve a toast! Do you remember when we met?

JANE. Oh, Porter –

PORTER. It was at Whalom Park, this was before it got burned down, and I was with my girlfriend at the time, Lesley –

JANE. – Who was very ugly –

PORTER. – She was called Ugly Lesley, yes, but she was still pretty in her way. And we were having our caricatures done. And Lesley, she was drawn as a football player, and she was throwing this football, but on the football was my face, and I was smiling, like I was really happy to be thrown. And I was sort of worried about how it was gonna look. Because on caricatures they have to…

JANE. Exaggerate the features –

PORTER. – To exaggerate the features, and I was worried about my nose…and my ears. I guess I've always been sort of…

JANE. Self-conscious about your appearance.

PORTER. But when I looked at my face on that football… I saw it, and for the first time, I could understand how someone could possibly, conceivably, find me attractive. And I asked that caricaturist, I said: What is your name? And she said –

JANE. Jane.

PORTER. And from then I knew: you were the best artist I'd ever met. And also. The love of my life.

> (JANE *and* PORTER *cheers. They drink. The wine is disgusting.* JANE *spits it out.*)

JANE. No way.

> *(They hug.)*

Shh. Can you hear that?

PORTER. What?

JANE. That is the sound of my career officially taking off! It's taking off, and I'm right behind it, and I'm running, I'm running so damn fast, and the sun is on my skin and I can see the mountains and the rivers and the trees! And the trees are all willows! And they are chuckling! Can you hear it, Porter?

(JANE *begins to laugh.*)

They are chuckling and cackling and snickering! The willows are laughing until they all choke!!

## Scene Two

*(Night. **JANE** eagerly works at her drawing board. **KING TOT** and **HOREMHEB** appear in the three-panel construct.)*

*(Panel One.)*

**KING TOT**. Horemheb. I am very irritated. Where is my sphinx cub?!

**HOREMHEB**. King Tot, the sphinx does not want to give up its child. Three dozen soldiers have been slain –

*(Panel Two.)*

**KING TOT**. I don't care. I want a sphinx cub and I want it now.

**HOREMHEB**. There's blood everywhere!

*(Panel Three.)*

**KING TOT**. I'll name it Samuel the Sphinx and it will lick my toes.

**HOREMHEB**. What a *cat*-astrophe!

*(Next comic. Panel One. **KING TOT** holds a pet sphinx.)*

This sphinx is an ancient and powerful being! To do this is like keeping a god as a pet!

**KING TOT**. Are you saying I'm not responsible enough to keep gods as pets?

*(Panel Two.)*

**HOREMHEB**. I just think that –

**KING TOT**. Horemheb –

**HOREMHEB**. Oh no, not again!

*(Panel Three.)*

**KING TOT**. I WANT MY MUMMY!

*(**JANE** finishes inking. **HOREMHEB** and **KING TOT** exit. **JANE** holds up her finished page. She smells it.)*

*(She puts the page on the large stack of other pages in the nearby tray. She turns off her drawing lamp and exits.)*

*(After a few moments, **ATLANTA** enters from outside. She carefully looks around, then crosses the room and exits. She returns, her arms laden with many bottles of Egyptian wine. She goes over to **JANE***'s work station.)*

*(**ATLANTA** picks up a bottle of India Ink. She holds it over **JANE***'s pile of comic strips. She pours the ink over the pages. She picks up the bottles of wine and exits to the outside.)*

## Scene Three

(**KISSY** *enters.*)

**KISSY**. Ding dong! Hello? Jane? Your door was unlocked so I welcomed myself right in! Jane! Oh Jane. Jaaaaane!

(**JANE** *enters.*)

**JANE**. Kissy Candida.

**KISSY**. Oh my God. Stop. Stop right where you are. Do not move an inch. Can you believe it?! Both of us nominated?? Such serendipity!

**JANE**. Right –

**KISSY**. But more like, more like, more like serenstripity! Serenstripity! Because we make, because we make comic strips! Serenstripity!

(**KISSY** *laughs at her joke.*)

This must be so *unexpected* for you! I mean when I saw you were nominated I was so *surprised!*

**JANE**. Oh, me too –

**KISSY**. No, I mean I was like *really, really* surprised.

**JANE**. ...Why were you so surprised?

**KISSY**. It's just, no offense, but if you look at me with "Summer Cramp" which is about, you know, real issues, like friendship and camping, and then you look at "King Tot" it just seems a little...and, well...how many panels does your strip have again?

**JANE**. ...Three.

**KISSY**. Right, and "Summer Cramp" has four so I mean... Oh, it doesn't mean my strip is more professional, or takes more effort; I'm just so surprised! Good for you! Pat yourself on the back! Go on. Pat it. Pat yourself on the back. Do it. Jane, do it.

(*Beat.* **JANE** *pats herself on the back.*)

So, three months of unpublished material! Gosh! Are you sweating? Show me your pits. Open up your pits.

JANE. I'm not showing you my pits.

KISSY. Bet they're like a water slide. Bet I could go tubing in there!

JANE. I'm set.

KISSY. ...You're set? You have it? Three months? Unpublished material?

JANE. Yeah.

KISSY. Huh.

JANE. How're you doing?

KISSY. Oh, I'm...you know, I have ideas. This head is like a, oh my Gosh, it is like an idea factory, like they're making triangle shirts in there! I'm thinking that the girls from Bunk Kabinapek are challenged to a s'more making competition, but watch out because Counselor Courtney might find herself in a pretty *sticky* situation!

> (KISSY *can't stop herself from laughing.*)

Oh my Gosh. Oh my Gosh. So much whimsy. Isn't it good to be friends?! So look: What do you think of Jeffica Newhart?

JANE. ...She's fine, I guess –

KISSY. Oh come on. Really? Jeffica Newhart? Lil' Lily? Please. It's so Christian, am I right? I mean, I'm a Christian, but it is like really Christian. Did you see that storyline about Lil' Lily baptizing her kitten? I think that's also blasphemy, by the way, and I don't think that's right for the Chuckling Willow, do you?

JANE. I guess not.

KISSY. Okay good, we're agreed. I don't care who wins as long as it's not Jeffica Newhart. But I have to warn you, I'm not going down without a fight, hahaha! Can I be honest with you, Jane? I'm hungry.

JANE. Do you want something to eat, or –?

KISSY. Oh no. I'm not hungry for food.

> (Beat.)

Anyway, I should probably be going –

JANE. Did you drive all the way here just to see me?

KISSY. ...I mean, it's really only an hour away if the traffic's good.

> *(Beat.)*

Maybe we should hug.

> *(They hug.)*

You are the salt of this earth Jane. I could just put you all over my French fries.

> *(**KISSY** exits. **JANE** shakes her head; she's about to return to work when **PORTER** enters. He appears shell-shocked.)*

JANE. Hey. You know who that was? Kissy Candida. Which reminds me, we need to start locking our doors –

PORTER. Hey Jane. Can you, uh...can you pass the wine?

JANE. You want a drink this early?

PORTER. I'd like the wine.

> *(**JANE** looks at **PORTER** oddly, then hands him the wine.)*

Thank you.

> *(**PORTER** drinks an enormous amount of wine.)*

JANE. Are you okay?

PORTER. This tastes so bad. This tastes so, so bad. Who is giving you this wine?!

JANE. Porter, what's wrong?

> *(Beat.)*

PORTER. I got a phone call just now.

JANE. Okay.

PORTER. It wasn't a normal phone call.

JANE. Porter –

PORTER. I don't know what a normal phone call is. But this wasn't one of those.

> *(Beat.)*

We uh. We have to go to the police station.

JANE. What? Why?

PORTER. It's about Atlanta…

JANE. Jesus. What did she do now?

PORTER. It's not. It's.

JANE. What is it?

PORTER. I guess I do know what a normal phone call is. I guess it's any phone call you don't think is strange.

JANE. Tell me right now.

>*(Beat.)*

PORTER. Last night. Last night. Atlanta went to Pattie's Donuts with Tracy and the, the girl with the thing on her chin. I don't remember her name but she…she has that thing on her chin. And they ordered three-dozen bear claws –

JANE. Three dozen –

PORTER. – The police said they were probably drunk. And then they…they went to the back parking lot, and Pattie has that pickup truck, that pickup truck with the sticker of the Celtics mascot peeing on the Statue of Liberty and they, they went up to the truck, and I don't know how they knew how to do this, but they siphoned the gasoline out of the truck. And then they began to… to drink the gasoline.

JANE. …What?

PORTER. And after they drank about…about twenty ounces each…they took off all their clothing. And lay naked in the back of the parking lot. Except for the girl with the thing on her chin. She was wearing her socks. Tweety Bird socks. They told me that.

I don't know why they told me that. And at approximately three o'clock this morning, in Pattie's parking lot, their bodies shut down, and they all died.

>*(JANE sits down on the floor.)*

So we have to, uh. Go to the police station.

>*(Beat.)*

Jane? Are you –

JANE. Shh.

> *(Beat.)*

PORTER. Do you want me to –

JANE. Don't say anything, please.

> (JANE *continues sitting on the floor.*)

PORTER. …Maybe you should get up off the ground?

JANE. …Okay.

> (JANE *stands and sits at her work station. They sit for some time.*)

PORTER. Are…are you…is everything…

> *(They continue in silence.* JANE *notices the ink-soaked papers in the nearby tray. She holds up an inky page.)*

JANE. …All of my pages are destroyed.

PORTER. What? Oh, Jane. It was probably. I mean. It was most likely –

JANE. Don't say her name. It wasn't.

PORTER. I'm sorry, it's just –

JANE. Don't say her fucking name!

> *(Beat.)*

You know who it was? It was Kissy Candida. It must have been her. When she first came into the house –

PORTER. Uh –

JANE. Three months. Three months gone. Thirty strips a month. One-hundred-sixty strips. I think I did the math wrong. I don't care. Do you even know what happened in these strips? Do you even know how cute it was? King Tot got a pet sphinx. They went on adventures together. The sphinx had a diamond collar. And a silk ball of yarn. And a scratching post made out of money. He had a lisp. It was very cute. It was very, very cute. Do you have any idea how cute that was?!

PORTER. …It sounds pretty cute –

**JANE**. It was adorable! Kissy Candida! Kissy "Summer Cramp" Candida! No one cares if you have four panels Kissy Candida, if they all look like ass! I said it! Her drawings look like ass! Her drawings look like she draws them with her ass! Like she sticks a pencil in her ass and draws!

**PORTER**. Janie –

**JANE**. I'm sorry, but I am expressing an opinion that Kissy Candida is a pencil-in-the-ass pervert! Do you have an issue, with that Porter?!

**PORTER**. …No.

**JANE**. Get me a pen. Get me India ink. Three months. I need to make up three months of work.

**PORTER**. Jane, I don't think I gave you this news well –

**JANE**. India ink!

> (**PORTER** *hands* **JANE** *a pen and India ink.* **JANE** *begins to draw. Her pen breaks.*)

I broke the pen.

> (**PORTER** *hands her another pen. She begins to draw. The pen breaks.*)

I broke the other pen.

**PORTER**. You're pressing down too hard –

**JANE**. What is wrong with these pens?! I think Kissy Candida sabotaged my pens! I think she put them up her ass!

> (**JANE** *buries her head in her hands.*)

**PORTER**. …Can we please stop talking about her behind? Let's… I know this isn't the best way to do this, but we really should go to –

**JANE**. No. You know what this is? An opportunity.

**PORTER**. What?

**JANE**. Because the strip could always be better. The strip could always be cuter. Maybe Samuel the Sphinx doesn't have a lisp. Maybe he has a different speech impediment. Maybe he can't pronounce his "L's." Like he says, "Hewwo." "Hewwo." I don't know, I'm thinking out loud. I have one week until the interview. I can make three months of strips in one week. That's possible. That's doable.

**PORTER.** I think you need to slow down –

**JANE.** Did Anne Frank slow down when she was running from the Nazis? Did Betsy Ross slow down when she was sewing the American flag? You know what else doesn't slow down? The Chuckling Willow. The Chuckling Willow doesn't slow down for any one. It's laughing, and laughing and I'm not going to let it down. I'm just not going to do that. Three months. One week. The best cartoonist in all of Eastern New England. It's too late to fail, Porter! It's too late to fall apart! Do you see what I'm saying?! Do you understand?!

   *(Beat.)*

It's too late for anything else.

## Scene Four

> (JANE *sits at her drawing board. She takes a deep breath. She begins drawing. The land is immersed in ink.* **KING TOT** *enters, very upset, drenched in black liquid.*)
>
> (*Panel One.*)

**KING TOT**. Horemheb! I am sticky! I am sticky and I do not like it!

**HOREMHEB**. Well I sure feel like a wet blanke–

> (JANE *crumples up the comic strip and begins a new one.* **HOREMHEB** *and* **KING TOT** *return to the first panel.*)
>
> (*Panel One.*)

**KING TOT**. Fuck. Fuck. Fuck. Fuck. Fuck –

> (JANE *crumples up the comic strip and begins a new one.* **HOREMHEB** *and* **KING TOT** *return to the first panel.* **JANE** *pauses. She begins to draw.*)
>
> (*Panel One.*)

**HOREMHEB**. You can do this. You can do this.

**KING TOT**. Hold it together.

> (*Panel Two.*)

**HOREMHEB**. Make a pun.

**KING TOT**. Don't think about it. Just make a pun.

> (*Panel Three.*)

**HOREMHEB**. Make a fucking pun.

**KING TOT**. Do it. Do it. Do it. You fucking scum. You fucking rancid pile of –

> (JANE *rips up the strip. As she does so, there's a sudden tear in the firmament of the panel construct.*)
>
> (*Panel One.*)

**HOREMHEB**. Have you heard the one about the writer who used too many words?

**KING TOT**. What?

*(Panel Two.)*

**HOREMHEB**. She was sentenced.

**KING TOT**. She was sentenced?

*(Panel Three.)*

**HOREMHEB**. She was sentenced to death.

(**JANE** *rips up the strip and begins again.*)

*(Panel One.)*

**KING TOT**. Horemheb! I am sticky and I do not like it! I did not decree that oil rain from the sky! The sands are black and wet and some of it got in my mouth and it tastes disgusting!

**HOREMHEB**. King Tot…I don't think this is oil…

**KING TOT**. What is it?

**HOREMHEB**. I don't know. But it is everywhere. The roofs are dyed black. Families have drowned in their quarters. The Nile looks like the night sky. The ibises and crocodiles are floating dead on the surface, their feathers and scales like stars.

*(Panel Two.)*

The scholars are calling it…the Great Black Nothing.

**KING TOT**. …the "Great Black Nothing"?

**HOREMHEB**. They say this blackness is a sign from the gods, a warning to you of your frivolous ways –

**KING TOT**. So now the gods think they can threaten me?!

*(Panel Three.)*

**HOREMHEB**. Do you want me to send for your royal prophets…?

**KING TOT**. No. I want… I want…

**HOREMHEB**. Oh boy…

**KING TOT**. I WANT MY MUMMY!!

> (**KING TOT**'s *scream is greater than it has ever been before.* **JANE** *viciously rips up another comic. This final rip, in conjunction with the scream, completely destroys the three-panel structure. And* **KING TOT** *and* **HOREMHEB** *emerge, free, from it.*)

Well?!

**HOREMHEB**. What?

**KING TOT**. I want my mummy!

> (*Beat.*)

**HOREMHEB**. I don't... I mean. Sire. You know I can't do that.

**KING TOT**. Why not?!

**HOREMHEB**. Oh...sire...Because she's dead.

**KING TOT**. ...What?

**HOREMHEB**. I mean she's...she's a mummy. She's in a tomb. She's dead.

**KING TOT**. Wait...I don't...how? How did this happen?

**HOREMHEB**. Well it...it's a very strange story, sire...when you were very young... One day she went into the royal gardens, and she...she plucked three bushels of pomegranates from a tree.

**KING TOT**. Three bushels of –

**HOREMHEB**. – We think she must have been under some divine influence or...she may have been drunk. And then, she went to the sewage pipe that passes through the gardens and...and somehow broke it open with her fingernails. And then she began to...to drink the sewage.

**KING TOT**. ...What?

**HOREMHEB**. And after she ingested God knows how much of the city's waste, she took off all of her robes, and her headdress, and her jewelry, and lay naked on the ground. And as the sun rose in the gardens of camellias and pomegranates, her body shut down. And she died.

*(Beat.)*

**KING TOT**. Bring me Samuel the Sphinx.

**HOREMHEB**. Samuel the Sphinx?

**KING TOT**. He will tell me a riddle. I will answer the riddle. And suddenly this will all make sense.

*(Beat.)*

GO!

*(**HOREMHEB** exits, then returns, carrying a mess of black feathers.)*

**HOREMHEB**. K-King Tot –

**KING TOT**. …What is that?

**HOREMHEB**. It's…Samuel the Sphinx.

**KING TOT**. …Put him down.

*(**HOREMHEB** puts the remains of Samuel the Sphinx on the ground. **KING TOT** suddenly starts kicking Samuel the Sphinx's remains.)*

**HOREMHEB**. Sire!

**KING TOT**. This sphinx is useless, Horemheb. Get it out of my sight.

**HOREMHEB**. Y-yes sire –

**KING TOT**. Throw it in the Nile. No feed it to the slaves. No feed it to the slaves then throw the slaves in the Nile –

**HOREMHEB**. Yes sire –

**KING TOT**. How many people have heard this story about my mother?

**HOREMHEB**. Well sire, it's sort of public knowledge –

**KING TOT**. Whoever knows this story, kill them. No one says her name or I cut out their tongues. No one thinks about her face or I cut off their heads. Search the city. And if anyone has the color of her hair, or the shape of her face, or the sound of her voice, burn them where they stand.

**HOREMHEB**. Yes sire.

*(HOREMHEB exits. PORTER enters; he does not look good. KING TOT exits.)*

**PORTER.** Hey.

**JANE.** Guess how many strips I've done. Guess.

**PORTER.** ...What?

**JANE.** Four weeks' worth. Fully inked. Got another week's worth of outlines. Bam. That's how it's done. Am I sleeping much? No. Does that matter? No. Ask me if they're any good.

**PORTER.** ...Are they any good?

**JANE.** I think it's the best work of my life.

**PORTER.** Huh.

**JANE.** I think it's my opus. I think it's my *Little Women.* I think it's my *Diary of Anne Frank.* I think it's my *Bible of King Tot.* Ask me how I'm doing this.

**PORTER.** How?

**JANE.** I don't know. I'm just going to keep doing it. Because my brain feels like a house on fire and I'm not going to slow down.

*(PORTER gets a bottle of wine.)*

I thought you didn't like that wine.

**PORTER.** I don't.

*(He drinks the wine.)*

...I spoke with the funeral director... Jane?

*(JANE doesn't look up.)*

And I have a, uh, a list. Of things I should ask you about. Okay?

*(PORTER takes out a notepad.)*

They want to know what dress she should wear. And I'm not...I'm not very good with clothes. So I thought maybe you could help with that? Jane?

**JANE.** ...What kind of sound effect do you think a dagger would make? "Thunk"? Or "Stab"? Which sounds funnier?

**PORTER.** …Thunk.

**JANE.** Thank you.

**PORTER.** …And they want some of her, um, her undergarments. Her under-things. For her to wear. And I don't know where she keeps them.

**JANE.** What do you think are funnier: frogs or toads?

**PORTER.** Janie, please –

**JANE.** Frogs or toads?

**PORTER.** …Frogs.

**JANE.** Frogs.

**PORTER.** Please I. I want you to get her underwear. Jane…?

**JANE.** …It looks like you're out of wine. Maybe you should get some more.

> *(A beat.* **PORTER** *gets another bottle of wine.* **JANE** *returns to her work.)*

**PORTER.** …Something else you should know. There was a problem. Because she didn't fit in the child casket. But the adult casket cost a lot more. Because it's made of oak. So they wanted to break her legs. So that she could fit in the child casket. And I said no. But, they had…they had already done it.

> *(***JANE*** *stops drawing.)*

So her…her legs are now broken. So we should probably pick a dress that covers her legs. And Tracy's parents, and the parents of the girl with the thing on her chin, they want to do a, uh, a joint funeral. With all three girls. As a community thing. And it costs less. That's what they said. I didn't bring up the cost. They want to know what date would be good? Jane? What date would be good?

**JANE.** I…any date. Any date is fine.

**PORTER.** There's, um, there's one more thing. And I don't know if I should… I considered not telling you, but…

> *(***PORTER*** *takes out a black cardboard box about the size of a softball.)*

**PORTER.** This came in the mail for you today. It's from Atlanta.

**JANE.** ...What?

**PORTER.** That's what it says, anyway. She must have put it in the mail before she...you know.

> *(Beat.)*

Are you going to open it?

**JANE.** No.

**PORTER.** Do you want me to open it?

**JANE.** No.

**PORTER.** Okay. Well I'm just going to, I'm just going to put it here. And when you're ready. When we're ready. Together. We'll open it. How does that sound?

> (**PORTER** *places the box down on a table.*)

Jane? How does that sound?

**JANE.** ...Okay.

**PORTER.** Just tell me. Please. Tell me that you'll pick out her underwear.

**JANE.** ...I'll pick out her underwear.

**PORTER.** You have no idea how much that means to me.

## Scene Five

(JANE *draws at her workspace.* KING TOT *sits on his throne. His hands are bloody; he has two buckets. One is full of frogs, the other is full of frog corpses. He's holding his knife and a frog's corpse.* HOREMHEB *enters, holding a bottle of Egyptian wine.*)

HOREMHEB. Sire, we've, um, we've gone through the city and…removed the women who bear any resemblance to –

KING TOT. The sands are still black Horemheb. I told you to remove the stains from the sands. And this stain. I cannot remove this stain from my skin.

(KING TOT *looks at the black mark on his lower arm, created by* ATLANTA*'s Sharpie markers.*)

HOREMHEB. Sire, we have all our slaves working tirelessly on removing the stains, but it's a very long process. The um, the other kingdoms of the ancient world have refused to send aid. But they did send this. I told your advisors… I said it wasn't appropriate for a nine-year-old boy, but –

(PORTER *presents* KING TOT *with a bottle of Egyptian wine.* KING TOT *kills a frog.*)

Sire… Did you…did you kill that frog?

KING TOT. I have a riddle. Samuel the Sphinx told it to me. I am the beginning of eternity, the end of time and space, the beginning of every end, the end of every place. What am I?

HOREMHEB. …What are you?

(KING TOT *puts the frog corpse in the bucket. He takes another frog and kills it.*)

KING TOT. I don't know. Samuel is gone and never told me what I was. Think of it this way. When I was born, my parents gave me the biggest present of all. This world is mine. The sky is mine. The sand is mine. And the frogs are mine too. So I will do with them as I please. In the same way, Horemheb, your bones belong to me; your skin belongs to me. When you breathe, I am the one permitting the air to enter into your lungs. And every time your heart beats, it is as king, "May I?" "May I?" And I am saying "Yes."

**HOREMHEB.** ...Thank you?

**KING TOT.** It's funny though. My dagger. I discovered a new use for it today.

> (**KING TOT** *removes a piece of the dagger's hilt, revealing that it is also a Sharpie marker.*)

Isn't that peculiar? Isn't that strange?

**HOREMHEB.** What...what is it?

**KING TOT.** Bend down to me Horemheb. I will show you.

> (**HOREMHEB** *bends down to* **KING TOT**. **KING TOT** *takes his Sharpie marker and begins drawing on* **HOREMHEB***'s neck.*)

Tell me. What do you know about the House of Osiris, Horemheb?

**HOREMHEB.** ...I, uh think only Anubis truly knows about the House of Osiris.

**KING TOT.** What do you know about the Great Black Nothing?

**HOREMHEB.** ...I think only Anubis truly knows about the Great Black Nothing.

**KING TOT.** There. I am finished.

> (**KING TOT** *has drawn a dotted line across* **HOREMHEB***'s throat with the Sharpie marker.* **HOREMHEB** *touches it.*)

**HOREMHEB.** I don't understand.

**KING TOT.** If I told you to kill yourself, Horemheb, would you do it?

**HOREMHEB.** To...to kill myself?

**KING TOT**. If you didn't you'd be disobeying a command. Would you disobey a command?

**HOREMHEB**. No. I would never do that.

**KING TOT**. So if I told you to, you'd kill yourself.

**HOREMHEB**. …I…yes. Yes, I would… Sire, maybe, maybe we could visit your diamond scarab collection, or go to your oasis of rubies –

**KING TOT**. Okay.

**HOREMHEB**. Okay?

**KING TOT**. Okay, that's all. That's all I wanted to know. You can leave, Horemheb.

>    (**HOREMHEB** *begins to leave.*)

Wait. Horemheb, come back.

>    (**HOREMHEB** *returns.*)

Take my dagger.

>    (**HOREMHEB** *takes the dagger.*)

Put it up to your throat.

>    (**HOREMHEB** *puts the dagger to his throat. Beat.*)

Close your eyes.

>    (**HOREMHEB** *closes his eyes.*)

Now tell me. What does it feel like?

**HOREMHEB**. I…

**KING TOT**. What is it like to be that close to the Great Black Nothing?

**HOREMHEB**. It feels like…business as usual.

>    (*Beat.*)

**KING TOT**. Okay. Give me my dagger. And also. The wine.

>    (**HOREMHEB** *hands* **KING TOT** *the wine.* **KING TOT** *looks at it. He takes a swig. He takes a piece of parchment. He draws on it with his Sharpie dagger, then hands it to* **HOREMHEB**.*)

Here. You can go now Horemheb.

**HOREMHEB**. What is this?

**KING TOT**. Plans.

**HOREMHEB**. What for?

**KING TOT**. My tomb.

> (**HOREMHEB** *exits, but* **KING TOT** *remains,*
> *continuing to kill frogs and drink wine.* **JANE** *stops*
> *drawing and picks up the black cardboard box.*
> *She looks at it.* **KISSY** *enters holding a stuffed bear.*
> **JANE** *puts down the box.*)

**KISSY**. …Hi. I went around to the community. Everyone.
Corey Peebler. Paul Moody. Jeffica Newhart. We bought
you this.

> (*She hands* **JANE** *the stuffed bear.*)

It's a stuffed bear. Squeeze it.

> (**JANE** *squeezes it.*)

…It's supposed to say something when you squeeze it.
I don't know why it isn't saying anything. It's supposed
to say: "We're there for you, Jane." …We're there for
you, Jane.

> (**JANE** *says nothing.*)

…When my mother died…she was old and it's not the
same, but still. When she died, I made a scrapbook.
And inside I put everything that reminded me of her.
Pictures and drawings and letters and recipes and…
when the funeral came, I read from her letters, and I
cooked her recipes, and…maybe that sounds silly. Or
trite or. But it helped me. It really did. So maybe that's
something I could help you with.

**JANE**. …I bet there was a lot of ink in that crap book, huh?

**KISSY**. What?

**JANE**. Ink. Because, I mean, you're a cartoonist. All those
letters. And drawings. And I know you like ink.

**KISSY**. …I guess there was ink in it.

**JANE**. Oh no, I mean, like a lot of ink. Like you really like
ink. In your dead mother's crap book.

**KISSY.** I'm sorry, are you...are you calling it a "crap book"?

**JANE.** I think I am, because you're full of shit.

**KISSY.** ...Excuse me?

**JANE.** I know that you sabotaged my comic strips you terrible little creature.

**KISSY.** Jane, I honestly have no idea what you're talking about –

**JANE.** Kissy, let me tell you something that has always bothered me about "Summer Cramp." The thing about "Summer Cramp" is that Counselor Courtney looks like a whore.

**KISSY.** What?

**JANE.** With her little camp shirt tied up to show her belly and her short shorts and her bullshit friendship bracelets –

**KISSY.** Counselor Courtney is an excellent role model –

**JANE.** For sluts. Oh, and by the way, the name "Summer Cramp"? "Summer *Cramp*"? That is a disgusting name –

**KISSY.** It's, it's like a leg cramp, because of all the hiking they do –

**JANE.** We both know it's all about menstruation you pathetic fucking liar!

**KISSY.** ...Jane, I know you're under a lot of stress, but I'm your friend and –

**JANE.** No. We're not friends.

**KISSY.** What?

**JANE.** We're not.

**KISSY.** Jane. I. I'm trying to support you. I know that you're upset because of your daughter –

**JANE.** I don't need your "support." You're lonely and petty and self-obsessed and if you talk about my daughter again I will take this pencil and shove it down your fat fucking throat.

(*JANE hands* **KISSY** *back the stuffed bear.*)

I don't want your bear. It doesn't even talk right.

*(Beat.)*

**KISSY.** I was talking to Lionel Feather the other day.

**JANE.** Excuse me?

**KISSY.** We went to dinner together.

*(JANE looks at her.)*

What? Everyone has to eat. Even Lionel Feather has to eat. The only thing is, when Lionel Feather eats, he eats lobster. That's right. We went to Red Lobster.

**JANE.** What did you talk about?

**KISSY.** Laughter. Comics. Massachusetts. Do you think I've had an easy life? Do you think I ever went to a camp like Camp Swimmahachee in "Summer Cramp"? Of course not. But the idea of this beautiful place with cabins, and lakes, and counselors who knew all these different clapping games…that sounds like a sort of heaven. It was a good conversation. Lionel and I will continue it at my interview. When he presents me with the Chuckling Willow. I'll see you at the funeral, Jane. And this time? I won't bring a bear.

*(KISSY exits.)*

## Scene Six

(JANE *draws.* KING TOT *enters with* ATLANTA*'s backpack. He dumps the contents of the backpack on the ground. Frog corpses spill from the bag. He takes a frog and stabs it with his dagger.* HOREMHEB *enters.*)

HOREMHEB. Sire, when I awoke this morning, there was a jackal sitting on my chest. And I couldn't breathe, and I started panicking and then...it was gone –

KING TOT. Horemheb, you are boring me.

HOREMHEB. And this afternoon, I saw the same jackal at the gates of our palace. And again, I felt a pressure on my chest and could not breathe...until it began to speak. Sire, the...the God of the Dead is here, and he'd like to talk to you.

KING TOT. ...Let him in.

(HOREMHEB *exits.* ANUBIS *enters.* KING TOT *sits on his throne and continues to kill frogs.*)

ANUBIS. Hello boy-king.

KING TOT. Hello Anubis.

ANUBIS. You cannot keep killing all these frogs.

KING TOT. Oh? Really?

ANUBIS. They are showing up at the House of Osiris. They make their way through the twenty-one pylons. The croaking is very loud. It's making it very hard to concentrate.

(KING TOT *kills another frog.*)

Boy-king...

KING TOT. I will keep killing the frogs. And when there are no more frogs left, I will kill the camels, then the crocodiles, then the cranes. And when the animals are gone, I will kill my slaves. And when the slaves are gone I will command all of my subjects to kill themselves, and the House of Osiris will be overwhelmed with croaking and chirping and chattering unless you listen to my demands.

**ANUBIS**. …What are your demands?

**KING TOT**. I WANT MY MUMMY!

>*(Beat.)*

I want my mother.

>*(Beat.)*

I'd like to see my mother again.

**ANUBIS**. Remove your crown.

**KING TOT**. …I am King Totankhamun, Amen-tot-ankh, Living Image of Amun, God-appointed ruler of Egypt!

**ANUBIS**. You are nine years old.

**KING TOT**. I am ageless!

**ANUBIS**. You are nine years old.

>*(Beat.* **KING TOT** *removes his crown.)*

I have talked to every creature that has ever existed. I have known them, and I have judged them. And I know you, and I will judge you. You are a very little boy who is very sad.

**KING TOT**. I am a divine ruler –

**ANUBIS**. And it was very unfair of life to put you in this position.

**KING TOT**. I own a sea. I am bathed by blind eunuchs, and feed my camels money –

**ANUBIS**. And for this, I am sorry, though it is no fault of my own. I cannot bring your mother to you. She is in the Fields of Aaru, now.

**KING TOT**. …How do I get to the Fields of Aaru?

**ANUBIS**. When you enter the House of Osiris, you must pass through the twenty-one pylons. And at each pylon, you will encounter a demon of malicious intent, armed with knives and teeth and fire, with bodies of women and heads of great beasts. You must recite the appropriate spells and pass their respective tests. And after you have completed this strange and terrible journey, you will come before me and my scales. Take out your heart, present it to me, and I will weigh it against an ostrich feather. And if your heart is pure, and you have committed none of the forty-two sins, then the scales will not tip. And then you may pass to the Fields of Aaru.

KING TOT. ...And if my heart weighs more than the ostrich feather?

ANUBIS. I will feed it to a Crocodile-Woman.

KING TOT. ...Anubis?

ANUBIS. Yes.

KING TOT. Do you like money?

ANUBIS. No.

KING TOT. I could teach you to like money. It's very easy to learn. And then I could give you lots of it. And then maybe you could –

ANUBIS. Stop talking.

KING TOT. Okay.

ANUBIS. Life is simple. Do not lie. Do not steal. And do not kill any more frogs.

> (ANUBIS *exits.* KING TOT *exits.* PORTER *enters with a bottle of wine.*)

PORTER. Jane? You uh...you wanted to practice for the interview –

JANE. Yes, I did. Thank you, Porter. You are on top of things and I appreciate it and I am ready like you would not believe. I have written out the ten most likely questions Lionel Feather will ask me in three days' time –

> (JANE *hands* PORTER *a piece of paper.*)

– Now it's essential that I present the platonic image of an Eastern New England humorist slash role model, and let me tell you, Lionel Feather may be funny but he's also fierce, like a clown who is also a lion. First question. Go.

PORTER. ...When did you begin cartooning?

JANE. I have always cartooned. I get up every day and I cartoon because it is who I am and what I do and I honestly consider that one of the primary reasons why my life has been a truly blessed affair. Next question.

PORTER. How would you respond to someone who said that women aren't funny?

JANE. I would spit in their face and laugh until I die. Next question.

PORTER. ...Did you, uh. Did you pick out her underwear?

JANE. ...That's not on the sheet.

PORTER. I'd just. I'd like to know. Did you do that?

JANE. ...Let's try to stick to the questions on the sheet –

PORTER. You haven't. Have you?

(Beat.)

Well you need to. 'Cause if you don't, she's gonna be buried without any underwear. She's gonna be naked under a dress that doesn't look good on her. With broken legs. And bugs crawling up her thighs.

JANE. I think you should stop drinking that.

PORTER. Next question: Why does the wine taste so bad? Because I think, I think that the woman from Wellfleet? Who sends you all of this? I think she's trying to poison you. I think she's trying to kill you. Because this is swill.

(PORTER finishes the wine and gets another.)

Next question? You ready for the next question?

JANE. Porter –

PORTER. How much do you actually know about Egyptian culture? Because everything you know seems to come from the first page of a Google image search. I read about Egypt. And in Egypt, in real Egypt, it's an absolute fucking disaster. It's all riots and racism and car bombs. All these pyramids you think are so cool? They were made by slaves. Real slaves, not like the one in your stupid white lady comic strip. And now the temples are all covered in graffiti from pissed off teenagers who hate where they're from. So tell me, do you even know anything about Egypt?

JANE. I know a lot of –

PORTER. And what is in that box? What is in that box because I don't know if you will, if you will ever be able to open it! Next question! On to the next question!

Can you draw a caricature of me anymore? Because I don't think you can. I think if I gave you a pencil and a piece of paper, you wouldn't know what to do, and it wouldn't look anything like me. And I think if I did a caricature of you, it wouldn't look like you, because apparently we don't know each other and I am so sad, I am so, so sad and you are not supporting me. You are not supporting me at all and I think you should know that.

    *(Beat.)*

JANE. I'm trying. I swear to God I'm trying. But it's very, very hard.

PORTER. We're burying our daughter in three days. It's a very hard time.

JANE. …The funeral is in three days?

PORTER. What?

JANE. …Nothing. No. It's just…that's the interview. That's my interview.

PORTER. …You said any date would be good. That's the date Tracy's mom wanted.

JANE. Can't you reschedule it?

PORTER. Can't you reschedule the interview?

JANE. But it's…it's Lionel Feather.

    **(PORTER** *begins to leave.)*

Wait. Porter. I… Please –

PORTER. Your character. Your slave in the comic strip. Is he supposed to look like me?

JANE. …No.

PORTER. He looks a lot like me.

JANE. It must be a coincidence.

PORTER. I'm kind of insulted by it.

JANE. I don't think you should be.

PORTER. Well, I am. I don't want you drawing him anymore.

(PORTER *exits.*)

## Scene Seven

(JANE *draws.* KING TOT *sits on his throne, morosely, drinking the Egyptian wine.*)

HOREMHEB. ...King Tot?

KING TOT. Hm?

HOREMHEB. Your tomb...your tomb is complete. I think. We made it to all of your specifications, but I don't... I'm not sure exactly how it works. Do you want me to... should I show it to you?

KING TOT. Yes, please.

(HOREMHEB *displays the tomb. It is the standing two-dimensional three-panel construct, but it's different from before. It now appears more like an Egyptian tomb wall.*)

HOREMHEB. I mean...where does the body go?

(KING TOT *stands in each of the three panels.*)

KING TOT. It goes here. Or here. Or here.

HOREMHEB. I don't think I understand –

KING TOT. My body will rest within these confines. Not moving. Not aging. Silent. Scentless. Perfect. On display. While those around me die and decay, while temples and kingdoms fall, I will be remembered forever. And that is how I will combat against the Great Black Nothing.

(KING TOT *takes out his dagger and examines it.*)

How long have we known each other, Horemheb?

HOREMHEB. Well, uh, sire, that would be nine years –

KING TOT. Yes. We have done many things together.

HOREMHEB. I went through a sandstorm to find you a ripe coconut. I built a sculpture of you out of diamonds and tiger bones. You bought and sold me many times over.

KING TOT. Yes, yes I did.

(Beat.)

**KING TOT**. Do you love me, Horemheb?

**HOREMHEB**. Of course, sire.

**KING TOT**. No. I mean, not as a servant…as a…as a friend.

**HOREMHEB**. …Sire…

**KING TOT**. Never mind. Don't answer that. It doesn't matter. Do you think I was a good king?

**HOREMHEB**. Oh, of course! Absolutely!

**KING TOT**. Are you lying, Horemheb?

**HOREMHEB**. I would never lie!

**KING TOT**. Please. Tell me the truth.

**HOREMHEB**. …I think you ruled a country as well as anyone could expect a nine-year-old boy to rule a country.

**KING TOT**. …Okay.

> *(Beat.)*

I think you may have been my friend. Don't tell me if you weren't, but I think you may have been.

> (**KING TOT** *draws a dotted line across his throat with the Sharpie dagger.*)

Take this dagger.

> (**KING TOT** *hands* **HOREMHEB** *the dagger.*)

**HOREMHEB**. Sire, please –

**KING TOT**. Put the dagger to my throat.

> (**KING TOT** *raises* **HOREMHEB**'s *hand so that the dagger is by his throat.*)

When I am gone, the next pharaoh will be Kheperkheperure. Burn all of my riches. Kill all of my slaves. They're mine, not his. Make sure the people still fear me. They can respect me. But make sure they fear me too. Tell them I was older than I am.

**HOREMHEB**. I think we should –

**KING TOT**. Take a hook. Stick it up my nose. Remove my brain through my nostrils. Cut an incision in the left side of my body. Take out my stomach. My liver. My intestines. And put them in jars. In their place, put

bags of sweet spices. Dry out my body for forty days.
Clean it with oil and brushes. Wrap it in many layers of
linen. Place me in three coffins. Then a sarcophagus.
Then put me in my tomb. Are you smart enough to
remember all that, Horemheb?

**HOREMHEB.** …Yes.

**KING TOT.** Now open me up.

> (**HOREMHEB** *holds the dagger to* **KING TOT**'s
> *throat. A moment. Then, he stands.*)

**HOREMHEB.** No.

**KING TOT.** Horemheb!

**HOREMHEB.** No. I can't. It's not. I'm not doing it.

**KING TOT.** You will do as I command! I am your king! You
are my slave!

**HOREMHEB.** King Tot. Listen. I know I am just one of
millions of slaves, I know this. But still, every day, when
you have a request or command… It's always me who
does your bidding. I don't know why, but it always is.
And I have watched you grow from something the size
of a small cat into this strange and beautiful creature
that stands in front of me now. And I know this is a
hard time. And I know there is nothing more difficult
than growing up. But if I don't try to stop this, I will
regret it every moment for the rest of my life.

> (*Beat.*)

**KING TOT.** Okay.

**HOREMHEB.** …Okay?

**KING TOT.** Okay.

**HOREMHEB.** Is that…is that it?

**KING TOT.** That's it.

> (**HOREMHEB** *hands* **KING TOT** *back his dagger.*)

Thank you.

> (*And suddenly* **KING TOT** *slashes his own throat
> with the knife. Black liquid begins to spill from the*

*wound.* **KING TOT** *gasps. He makes a terrible noise and looks, perplexed, at the ink on his hands.)*

**HOREMHEB.** No! No, no, no, no, no –

*(***HOREMHEB*** grabs* **KING TOT**'s *body and holds him close.* **KING TOT** *dies.)*

## Scene Eight

(JANE *enters, dressed fancier than we've seen previously. She prepares to leave.* PORTER *watches her.*)

PORTER. Funeral today.

JANE. Mm.

PORTER. Lots of people will wonder where you are.

JANE. Guess so.

PORTER. Lots of people won't understand.

JANE. Maybe.

(*Beat.*)

PORTER. I spoke to the mother of the girl with the thing on her chin.

(*Beat.*)

She has a thing on her chin too. But it's even bigger. It takes up like half her face. And I asked her if she… she had any idea about why they…did what they did. And she said that after…that night. She went on her daughter's computer…and she found this word document that said "My Suicide Note." Except "suicide" was misspelled. So she opened the word document. But it wasn't really a note. It was just three pictures. And the first picture was of the tennis player Serena Williams. And the second picture was of Atlanta, and Tracy, and the girl with the thing on her chin when they were in some school play dressed as these old men with beards. And the third picture was of Porky Pig saying, "That's all folks."

(*Beat.*)

And I'm trying…I'm trying to make sense of it. And I spent about four hours googling Porky Pig and Serena Williams. And then another hour googling Venus Williams, because I thought maybe I'd made a mistake. And I saw this one picture of Venus Williams when she was…she must've been only around six years old…and she was holding this tennis racket that was about as big as her…and she was smiling…she was smiling so big… and I realized…I don't know why they did it. I don't think I'm ever going to know why they did it.

(*Beat.*)

Please Jane. I know you blame yourself. But you have to let it go.

JANE. …I don't blame myself.

PORTER. Okay –

JANE. Was she depressed? She was a sixteen-year-old girl, of course she was depressed. But she had friends. And she did okay in school and I was her mother and mothers always see only the worst parts of their daughter so why should I have been worried? A week ago we saw a commercial with a talking cat and we both laughed. And when she thought I wasn't home, I could hear her singing in her room and she sounded fucking beautiful. And people who do what she did don't sound that good singing. So maybe you actually don't know anything at all.

PORTER. Maybe I don't.

(*Beat.*)

JANE. I opened the box that she sent.

PORTER. …You opened it without me?

JANE. Yes.

PORTER. …What was inside?

(JANE *picks up the box. She opens it. She holds it upside down. A large rock falls out.*)

JANE. What the fuck. What the fuck is wrong with her?! Seriously, what the fuck kind of move is that?!
That's bullshit! That's evil fucking bullshit! And I don't know what I did to deserve this! Because fuck her! Fuck her! Fuck her!

PORTER. …Jane. Please. Come to the funeral.

(JANE *turns away from* PORTER.)

Jane?

(*Beat.*)

Jane?

(JANE *addresses the audience.* PORTER *exits.*)

JANE. At the First Pylon of the House of Osiris, one shall meet the Doorkeeper Neruit, Insect-Headed, Lady of Tremblings, high-walled, who uttereth the words which drive back the destroyers. And one must pass her terrible trial, and still one must wander on.

(KING TOT *stands in the first panel of his tomb.*)

JANE & KING TOT. At the Second Pylon of the House of Osiris, one shall meet the Doorkeeper Mes-Ptah, Goat-Headed, Mistress of the Two Lands, devourer by fire, who art greater than any human being. And one must pass her terrible trial, and still one must wander on.

(KING TOT *moves to the second panel.*)

At the Fifth Pylon of the House of Osiris one shall meet the Doorkeeper Nekau, Baboon-Headed, Prevailer with Knives, Lady of Hair, who decreeth the release of those who suffer through evil hap. And one must pass her terrible trial, and still one must wander on.

(KING TOT *moves to the third panel. A pair of chairs.* KISSY *sits in one of them.*)

KISSY. Hi Jane.

JANE. Hey.

KISSY. Are you nervous? I'm not nervous. Do you know why? Because of something Lionel Feather said to me in bed yesterday.

(JANE *looks at* KISSY.)

What? Lionel Feather has a bed. Everyone has a bed. The only thing is, when Lionel Feather sleeps, he sleeps on water. That's right. It's a water bed.

**KING TOT.** At the Tenth Pylon of the House of Osiris one shall meet the Doorkeeper Sekhenur, Hippopotamus-Headed, Goddess of the Loud Voice, the awful one who terrifieth, who herself remaineth unterrified within. And one must pass her terrible trial, and still one must wander on.

>     (**KING TOT** *returns to the first panel.*)

**KISSY.** Anyway, Lionel turned to me and he said, "Kissy Candida, the truth about humor is this: the funniest people are always the most sad. But the trick is to be sad enough to be funny, but not sad enough to destroy your life." And I agree with this. Some of us are sad enough to be funny. And some of us are sad enough to destroy their life. And that's why I'm going to win the Chuckling Willow.

**KING TOT.** At the Eighteenth Pylon of the House of Osiris one shall meet the Doorkeeper Whose Name is Not Known, Scorpion-Headed, lover of slaughterings, cutter of heads, slaughterer of fiends at eventide. And one must pass her terrible trial, and still one must wander on.

>     (**KING TOT** *moves to the second panel. We begin to hear the croaking of frogs.*)

**KISSY.** You're a bad person, Jane. I look at you. And to be honest? It makes me sick.

>     (**KISSY** *makes a puking noise.*)

You're bad. You're a bad thing.

>     (**KISSY** *makes another puking noise.*)

Your head is bad your heart is bad you hurt yes your heart hurts but you're bad and I'm hungry so hungry I am hungry beyond all belief.

>     (*Beat.* **KISSY** *makes another puking noise.*)

Would you excuse me for a second?

>     (*She turns to a corner.*)

KING TOT. At the Twenty-first Pylon of the House of Osiris, one shall meet the Doorkeeper –

> (*And then* KING TOT *sees* KISSY *huddled in the corner, puking.*)

…Hello?

> (KISSY *turns to* KING TOT. *She is now the* CROCODILE-WOMAN. *She wipes her mouth.*)

CROCODILE-WOMAN. Hi what are you oh my hello little lost boy-thing yum yum yum.

KING TOT. …Are you the Crocodile-Woman?

> (*The* CROCODILE-WOMAN *approaches* KING TOT *in a predatory way.*)

CROCODILE-WOMAN. Eat them eat hearts hearts eat hurts everything that ever hurts I eat yum yum yum. Do you hurt? Do you hurt?

KING TOT. …What?

CROCODILE-WOMAN. Do you hurt, boy-thing?

KING TOT. I…I don't know –

> (*The* CROCODILE-WOMAN *holds her stomach. She might puke again. She stops herself.*)

CROCODILE-WOMAN. Hungry so hungry always hungry my stomach is limitless because the badness in all men is limitless can I lick your skin can I lick your skin to get to your heart yum yum yum –

KING TOT. Stop it!

CROCODILE-WOMAN. Inside of you is sewage rotten pomegranate bear claws ripping at your chest wine so much wine wine enough to make a kingdom drunk and tears so many tears so many tears because you existed little boy-thing yum yum yum. Let me lick your skin. I will be delicate. But it will still hurt very, very much.

> (*The* CROCODILE-WOMAN *is about to lick* KING TOT*'s skin.* ANUBIS *enters and sits on his throne.*)

**ANUBIS.** Crocodile-Woman. That is our guest. You cannot lick his skin.

(*The* **CROCODILE-WOMAN** *mopes and exits.*)

Hello boy-king.

**KING TOT.** ...Hello Anubis.

**ANUBIS.** You have met my Crocodile-Woman.

**KING TOT.** Yes, I have.

**ANUBIS.** She has been eating all of your frogs. They croak inside of her stomach.

**KING TOT.** So this is it? This is the House of Osiris? Where are the columns? Where are the murals?

**ANUBIS.** King Tot.

**KING TOT.** Where are the statues?! Where are the gems and the gold and the –

**ANUBIS.** King Tot. Be silent.

(*The* **CROCODILE-WOMAN** *re-enters with the scale. On one side of the scale is an ostrich feather.*)

I need your heart.

**KING TOT.** Right. About that. I sort of have a question.

**ANUBIS.** Yes?

**KING TOT.** If my heart is heavier than the ostrich feather. And I'm not saying it is. But if it is. And she devours it –

**CROCODILE-WOMAN.** Yum, yum, yum –

**KING TOT.** – Then... What happens next? What happens to me?

**ANUBIS.** What happens next is this. Your heart is gone. You are gone.

**KING TOT.** What does that mean, "gone"?

**ANUBIS.** It means gone, boy-king. It means what it has always meant.

(*Beat.*)

**KING TOT.** Okay.

(*Beat.* **KING TOT** *reaches into his chest. He makes a weak sound. He pulls out his heart. It is the black rock that* **ATLANTA** *sent in the mail.*)

…Is this it?

(**ANUBIS** *reaches over and takes his rock.*)

ANUBIS. It is smaller than most think. We begin life with a heart as light as a cough. And though our bones may grow, and our skin may stretch, our heart does not. King Tot. Have you committed even one of the forty-two sins that would lie heavy upon your heart?

KING TOT. No.

ANUBIS. Well let us see.

(**ANUBIS** *places the rock upon the scale. The rock is so heavy that the scale immediately breaks. Beat. The* **CROCODILE-WOMAN** *is delighted.*)

(*Beat.*)

KING TOT. I think your scale doesn't work right.

ANUBIS. This scale was made at the beginning of all time to judge the worthiness of men.

KING TOT. Well I think it's broken.

(**ANUBIS** *picks up* **KING TOT**'*s heart.*)

ANUBIS. Crocodile-Woman –

KING TOT. Wait! Anubis. Wait. What do you want? What do you need? I have lots of things –

ANUBIS. I need nothing but my position.

KING TOT. I will give you my kingdom. I will give you my clothes. I will come to you as a beggar with nothing but my eyes and mouth and hair! I will give you my hands. I will give you my words. I will give you my youth and my teeth and my knowledge –

ANUBIS. Oh, boy-king.

KING TOT. What?

ANUBIS. You believe yourself to have so many, many things. But look upon yourself. You are such a frail, delicate creature. You are but a caricature up on the crumbling wall that is creation. And the universe shudders, bends, and breaks with but a single word. Do you know what that word is?

KING TOT. ...No.

ANUBIS. "Next."

    *(Beat.)*

KING TOT. What?

ANUBIS. Next.

KING TOT. I'm confused.

ANUBIS. Next?

    *(Beat.)*

Next?

    **(ANUBIS** *stands and walks to where* **JANE** *sits.)*

Are you deliberately ignoring me?

JANE. Oh! Mr. Feather! I'm, I'm so sorry! I guess I was sort of in my head –

ANUBIS. Please, enter.

    *(He returns to his throne.* **JANE** *follows.)*

JANE. This is, uh, it's a very nice room –

ANUBIS. It costs two hundred dollars a night.

JANE. Right. Well, Mr. Feather, can I just say what an absolute honor it is to meet you. I mean, I grew up reading "Packrats" –

ANUBIS. Yes. "Packrats." Five abandoned children, forced to fend for themselves in a junk yard. But they do not fall apart. They do not descend into savagery. They forge friendships and have delightful misadventures.

JANE. It's very inspiring –

ANUBIS. They feast on rats. They create chants. They make a clubhouse out of an old refrigerator.

JANE. It's very cute –

ANUBIS. It was based on my own childhood.

> (JANE *laughs awkwardly.*)

That was not a joke. I was homeless from age three to thirteen.

JANE. ...I'm so sorry.

ANUBIS. My stomach is scarred with bites from unknown nocturnal creatures.

JANE. ...Was that a joke?

ANUBIS. I've never said a joke in my entire life.

> (*Beat.*)

JANE. I'm sorry, I just, let me collect myself –

ANUBIS. Ms. Haley. I have questions to ask of you. Do you feel prepared to answer them to the best of your ability?

JANE. Absolutely.

ANUBIS. When did you begin cartooning?

JANE. I have always cartooned. I get up every day and I cartoon because it is who I am and what I do and I honestly consider that one of the primary reasons why my life has been a truly blessed affair.

ANUBIS. Has it been?

JANE. Excuse me?

ANUBIS. Blessed. Have you been blessed?

> (*Beat.*)

JANE. Yeah. I mean. I think... God is... I think we're all blessed. Just to be here. Just to experience this. Yes.

ANUBIS. For three decades I have been the highest authority on Eastern New England cartooning. And during this time I have created an impenetrable set of forty-two criteria by which I judge a comic strip. This morning, I read through your three months of "King Tot" strips and assigned to them a score ranking between zero and forty-two. Would you like to know that score?

JANE. ...Yes.

ANUBIS. Twelve.

**JANE**. …Twelve?

**ANUBIS**. Twelve.

**JANE**. I…I don't understand.

**ANUBIS**. Twelve.

**JANE**. No, I get that –

**ANUBIS**. Your drafting is shoddy. Your inking is subpar. Your story line is challenging to follow. And I didn't laugh.

**JANE**. You didn't laugh?

**ANUBIS**. I didn't laugh.

**JANE**. …Do you want to hear a joke?

**ANUBIS**. I would like that, yes.

**JANE**. It's more of a riddle, actually. I am the beginning of eternity, the end of time and space, the beginning of every end, the end of every place. What am I?

**ANUBIS**. I don't know. What am I?

**JANE**. You're a fucking asshole.

**ANUBIS**. Excuse me?

**JANE**. You're a fucking asshole who lived in a dump. I heard about you. I know what you're really judging. And it's not what's on the page. It's what's in the fucking bedroom.

So I have an interview question for you, "Lionel Feather": How many of these women have you fucked with your old ass wrinkled dick?!

**ANUBIS**. …I don't appreciate you commenting that way about my genitalia.

**JANE**. Yeah, so, so, here's what I think. I think you've wasted my time. I think you've wasted your life. I think it's all shitty and worthless and dumb and you have no idea what's actually meaningful or important. If the Chuckling Willow was a person, I'd beat it to death. If the Chuckling Willow was a tree, I'd burn it to the ground. Because I hate you so much, and I hate her so much, and I hate myself more than I ever fucking thought possible. Because she was asking me, she was begging me not to let her go to Tracy's, and I let her down. And the thing is, I swear to God she fucking loved me. Even if she was a horrible fucking bitch about it. Even if I was an incompetent piece of crap. We both loved each other more than makes sense and fuck anyone else who thinks otherwise.

> (**JANE** *slumps back, exhausted.*)

> (**KING TOT** *has watched the entirety of* **JANE***'s scene. Finally, he speaks.*)

**KING TOT.** Anubis. Do you have a mother?

**ANUBIS.** My mother is Nephthys, whose voice sounds like the cries of a hawk, and who appears to the dead as a woman with wings instead of hands.

**KING TOT.** Did you know her?

**ANUBIS.** Yes. She haunts me daily.

**KING TOT.** Okay. Well, I don't think I…I don't think I… knew my mother, enough. As well as I want to and this…the scale. The heart. It isn't fair.

**ANUBIS.** What do you mean?

**KING TOT.** This scale is made to judge the worthiness of men. But I'm not a man.

> (*Beat.*)

**ANUBIS.** I have watched your actions from here, the House of Osiris for many years. I have seen you waste masses of wealth on absurd frivolities. I have seen you build palaces while your kingdom starves. How do you think I react to these things?

**KING TOT.** …I don't know.

**ANUBIS.** They amuse me. I do not laugh. But I am amused.

**KING TOT.** …Oh.

**ANUBIS.** It is a sort of morning ritual of mine. To watch your antics. Before I begin my day. I particularly liked the lisping sphinx. And in this world, brief amusement, it has worth. Not much. But some.

**JANE.** …Thank you.

**ANUBIS**. South of the Mediterranean Sea, there is an area of Egypt called "the black land." And in this black land, there is a tree. A willow. And this willow, it makes a sound. A strange sound. A sound impossible to understand. Typically, you see, willows weep. But weeping is actually very, very similar to chuckling. One thing is certain, though. Whether it be from grief or joy, tears flow from the willow's wood. And from these tears, plants grow, lotuses, and papyri, and date palms, with fruit that hangs like lungs. And the tears, they flow down the banks of the black land and form a stream, and from the stream forms a river. And we call this river The Nile, which means "Great River," but also "The Light of One's Open Face." Do you see what I am saying?

**JANE & KING TOT**. No.

**ANUBIS**. Out of a possible forty-two points, you received twelve. I am a severe judge, this is true. And no other cartoonist received above a ten.

**JANE**. …What?

**ANUBIS**. You have insulted me. You have flaws, great in size and depth. But I will give you one gift for that which you have given me. And that gift is indifference. You may go to the Fields of Aaru. The prize is yours to have. If this is what you want.

>            (JANE *leaves.*)

**KING TOT**. …Um. What about my heart?

**ANUBIS**. I must admit. I am loath to feed it to my Crocodile-Woman. I think she is sick from eating so many frogs.

**KING TOT**. …Can I have it?

>            (**ANUBIS** *considers and hands* **KING TOT** *the rock.*
>            **KING TOT** *exits.*)
>
>            (*Beat.*)
>
>            (**KING TOT** *re-enters, stands in the first panel.*)

The Fields of Aaru are situated in the East, where the sun is eternally rising. It appears as a land of endless reeds stretching out into the infinite, that sway gently and in great synchronicity. And those who have overcome the terrible challenges of the world arrive and are greeted by –

(JANE *enters. She's a* MUMMY.)

...Hi.

MUMMY. ...Hi.

KING TOT. ...Are you for real?

MUMMY. Yeah.

KING TOT. I'm sorry. I'm sorry about everything. But I wasn't... I just wasn't...

MUMMY. I should've come earlier. I'm sorry I didn't come earlier.

KING TOT. ...I got you something.

(KING TOT *takes out the rock.*)

I made it myself.

(*He hands it to the* MUMMY.)

...Is it heavy?

MUMMY. Yeah. It is.

### The End